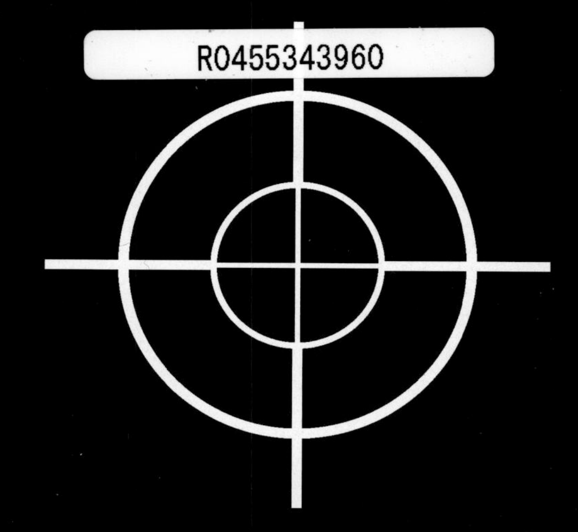
R0455343960

D1417942

Explore
NOT FAR. WON'T BE LONG.
AND I WILL BE THE ONE... TO HOLD YOU DOWN... KISS YOU SO HARD...
I WILL... TAKE YOUR BREATH AWAY.

LATE.

YOU'RE LATE.
HARD PLACE TO FIND.
CAN I TAKE OFF THE HOOD NOW?
NO.
YOU CAN LEAVE NOW.
TELL JON I'LL CALL HIM.

I KNOW EVERYTHING ABOUT YOU, MOLLY. YOU HAVE NO SECRETS HERE. NOT FROM ME. REMEMBER THAT. MAKE IT THE FIRST RULE OF YOUR NEW LIFE HERE.

OKAY.
CAN I TAKE OFF THE HOOD NOW?
NO.

YOU CAN STAY HERE. IN MY SON'S OLD ROOM. EDEN ISN'T A PLACE YOU SPLASH. IT'S A PLACE YOU WADE INTO.
I'LL PREPARE YOU FOR OUR TOWN. AND I'LL PREPARE THE TOWN FOR YOU.
IT'S HOT UNDER THIS HOOD, MA'AM.

YOU CAN TAKE IT OFF.
WELCOME TO EDEN.

THANK YOU FOR HELPING ME.

SHE'S HERE. I'M KEEPING HER IN THE HOUSE WITH ME.
THE ARMENIANS ARE LOOKING FOR HER, BUT THEY WON'T COME TO EDEN.
EDEN'S A STRONG PLACE. YOU SURE SHE'S A STRONG GIRL?
SHE'S STRONG ENOUGH.
KEEP HER SAFE, LAURA.
YEAH.

REDUCE THE INFORMATION. TO ONLY WHAT IS ESSENTIAL. EVERYTHING LEAVES A TRACE. FIND IT.
THERE ARE BROKEN STICKS AROUND THE MIDDLE TREE. ONLY THE MIDDLE TREE.
CENTER TREE. FOUND YOU.
YOU CAN COME OUT NOW.

HOW?
YOU CHEATED. YOU OPENED YOUR EYES.
I DID NOT.
I SAW THE DETAILS --
YOU SAW THE DETAILS AND THEY TOLD YOU WHAT I DID.
FIVE TIMES IN A ROW. YOU PLAY HIDE AND GO SEEK LIKE THIS AS A KID?
I ONLY PLAYED HIDE AND GO SEEK ONCE. NO ONE CAME TO FIND ME.
SEE, NOW YOU TOLD ME THE SAD THING AND I CAN'T BE MAD AT YOU FOR WINNING. WELL PLAYED.

I'M USING HUMOR TO DISARM YOU SO YOU FIND ME MORE ATTRACTIVE.
IT DOESN'T WORK AS WELL WHEN YOU EXPLAIN IT.
I'LL MAKE NOTE OF THAT.
I'M A PROJECT. HOW ROMANTIC.
IT'S A NICE MORNING. WALK ME INTO TOWN.
OKAY.

Made you breakfast, Miss Mayor
SHE DIDN'T.
MOLLY?
Beautiful day. Went for a walk
WALK.
RIGHT.

I'LL TAKE YOUR BREATH AWAY...I'LL HOLD YOU DOWN...
NICE VOICE.

YOU KNOW WHAT THEY SAY ABOUT GIRLS WHO SING?
THEY SAY IT'S EASY TO MAKE THEM SCREAM.
JUST A LITTLE TOUCH WILL DO.
EXCUSE ME--
WHY YOU RUNNING OFF?
I'M SORRY, I--
LANCE.

STOP THE MADCAPPIN'. LEAVE HER BE.
LEAVE HER BE.
I WAS JUST...TALKING, MAGGIE--
I'M GONE.
I'M MAGGIE. MAYOR SHIFFRON MENTIONED A NEW MOVE-IN.
THERE'S NO WELCOME WAGON, BUT THERE'S NO REASON TO FEEL ALONE.

HAPPY TO MEET YOU, MAGGIE.
YEAH. ABOUT THAT.
YOU NEED TO BE CAREFUL HERE.
PEOPLE HERE ARE MORE THAN WHAT THEY SEEM. OR LESS.
THAT GUY? LANCE. BEFORE HE CAME HERE HE HURT WOMEN. NOW HE THINKS ABOUT IT.
REALLY? OH GOD.
YEAH. HE KNOWS BETTER THAN TO OVERSTEP HIS BOUNDS, BUT DON'T BE THE MISTAKE HE GETS TO MAKE BEFORE JUSTICE COMES. YOU'RE YOUNG. PRETTY. NOT A LOT OF THAT HERE.
STAY OUT OF THE BARS. WATCH YOURSELF AT NIGHT. UNTIL YOU GET THE RHYTHM.
I WORK AT THE DINER. SEE ME SOMETIME.
LOOKS LIKE YOU'RE MY FIRST FRIEND, MAGGIE. THANK YOU.

ONE GIRL. NOT READY.

"THERE'S NOTHING TO EDEN, WYOMING."
GO TO GOOGLE MAPS AND ALL YOU'LL SEE ARE TREES. I DON'T THINK YOU TRANSFERRED HERE TO CHASE BIGFOOT AND THE LOCH NESS MONSTER.
FBI
LOCH NESS IS IN SCOTLAND, SIR. THIS CURIOSITY IS MORE LOCAL. IT'S WORTH A LOOK.
I DISAGREE. WE'VE GOT METH DISTRIBUTION RINGS ACROSS THE STATE AND MORE THAN A FEW RIGHT-WING GROUPS WITH TOO MANY GUNS AND TOO LITTLE SURVEILLANCE. YOU'VE GOT A GOOD RESUME, BREMBLE, AND I'D LIKE TO APPLY THAT TO THE REAL PROBLEMS WE HAVE, NOT THE RUMORS.
I APPRECIATE YOUR AUTHORITY, SIR. AND YOUR RESPONSIBILITY. THAT'S WHY I ALREADY SPOKE WITH WASHINGTON.

YOU SPOKE TO WASHINGTON.
YES, SIR. BEFORE I CAME TO WYOMING.
I WANTED TO GIVE YOU THE SPACE TO ALLOW AN INVESTIGATION. I'M CERTAIN THESE RUMORS MUST CONCERN YOU.

IT IS CONCERNING.
YOUR PATH IS CLEARED, SIR. I'LL FORWARD THE EMAIL FROM WASHINGTON.
MAYBE THERE'S NO "THERE" THERE. EITHER WAY, WE'LL FIND OUT.
IT SEEMS WE WILL, AGENT BREMBLE.

"SHIRLEY TEMPLE? HAVEN'T MADE ONE OF THOSE SINCE I GOT BEHIND THIS BAR."
BAR
McCarthy's
I NEVER DRINK. MAKES ME FOGGY. STINK COMES THROUGH THE SKIN. I JUST LIKE BARS. USED TO WORK IN ONE.
WE DON'T REALLY TALK ABOUT OUR LIVES BEFORE, HONEY. KEEPS THE AIR LIGHT.
WHO YOU ARE IS WHO YOU ARE HERE.
THAT'S A NICE RULE.
"KEEPS THE AIR LIGHT." I LIKE THAT.
YOU CAN'T BE AS DECENT AS YOU LOOK, HONEY.
NOBODY IS.

SCREAMER. MAYBE I CAN BUY YOU A DRINK.

YOU SHOULD LEAVE, MA'AM.

THE LIGHT AIR IS ABOUT TO GET HEAVY.

YOU SEEM NICE. TOO NICE FOR WHAT'S GOING TO HAPPEN NEXT.

MS. SHIFFRON...
I'M SCARED...
I'M SO SCARED...

"I LEFT THE MESS IN THERE BECAUSE I WANT YOU TO LOOK AT IT.
"SHE SAYS SHE WAS ATTACKED. BARTENDER TRIED TO HELP AND LANCE KILLED HER.
OPEN
"THEN SHE KILLED LANCE IN SELF-DEFENSE.
"I TRUST YOUR EYES, SON. TELL ME WHAT HAPPENED."
OPEN
FASCINATING.

"REDUCE THE INFORMATION --
"TO WHAT IS ESSENTIAL.
"EVERYTHING LEAVES A TRACE."
I SEE.
I DON'T WANT THE BARTENDER TO BE DEAD. SHE WAS NEVER CRUEL TO ME.
NOT ONCE.

EXCUSE ME.
MY MOTHER IS ASLEEP SO I'M SPEAKING QUIETLY.
YOU'RE THE SON?
I AM THE SON.
AND WHAT YOU SAID DIDN'T HAPPEN.
YOU KILLED THEM BOTH.

HMM.
WELL, MAYBE.
BUT HE WAS BAAAAD.
AND I DID TRY TO GET THE BARTENDER TO LEAVE.
YOU DIDN'T COME HERE TO TELL YOUR MOTHER. YOU CAME BECAUSE YOU'RE CURIOUS.
I AM CURIOUS ABOUT YOU.
THEN CLOSE THE DOOR.
AND YOU CAN ASK ME ANYTHING YOU WANT.

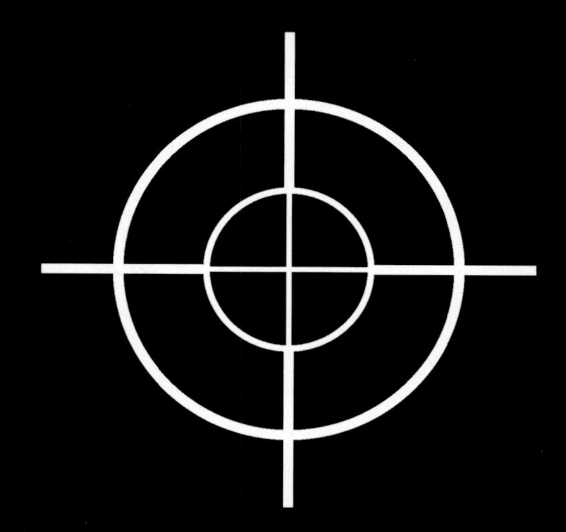

"I ASKED YOU TO TELL ME WHAT YOU THOUGHT. I DIDN'T ASK YOU TO TALK TO HER."
I THOUGHT YOU WERE ALL ABOUT SPECIFICS.
I AM.
YOU DIDN'T TELL ME NOT TO SPEAK WITH HER.
SO. YOU TALKED TO HER. WHAT DO YOU THINK?
YOU WANT TO KNOW WHAT SHE TOLD ME? OR WHAT I THINK ABOUT HER?
FUCK WHAT SHE TOLD YOU. I WANT TO KNOW WHAT SHE IS.
PEOPLE WOULD SAY WHAT SHE IS...IS COMPLICATED.
BUT I THINK IT'S PRETTY SIMPLE. SIMPLE THE SAME WAY A SHARK IS SIMPLE.

"SHE'S A SOCIOPATH. FROM WHAT I UNDERSTAND OF THE DEFINITION.
"SHE'S MANIPULATIVE AND PLAYS INTO THE WEAKNESSES OF OTHERS.
"YOU HAVE A DEAD DAUGHTER. MY DEAD SISTER. I BELIEVE MOLLY HAS KNOWLEDGE OF THAT AND USED IT.
"SHE ACTED LIKE A LITTLE GIRL FOR YOU.
"THEN SHE KILLED EVERYONE IN THE BAR. SHE ENGINEERED A SITUATION WHERE SHE COULD KILL.
"BECAUSE SHE ENJOYS KILLING.
"AS I SAID. SHARK SIMPLE.
"SHE'S THE KIND OF PERSON YOU NORMALLY ELIMINATE. I ASSUMED THAT IS WHAT YOU WOULD DO.
"SO I WANTED TO TALK TO HER FIRST.
"NOT MANY PEOPLE GET TO PET A SHARK."

THAT'S BECAUSE SHARKS AREN'T PETS.
SOME PEOPLE KEEP THEM AS PETS. THE SPECIES IS CALLED GINGLYMOSTOMA CIRRATUM AND THEY'RE KEPT INSIDE TANKS BALANCED FOR --
MARK.
SORRY.
I CAN'T ELIMINATE HER. DON'T ASK ME TO TELL YOU WHY BECAUSE I WON'T. IT'S NOT SOMETHING YOU NEED TO KNOW. JUST KNOW THAT I HAVE TO PROTECT HER.
DON'T BE CURIOUS ABOUT HER. STAY AWAY FROM HER.
OKAY.
SHE'S NOT THE ONLY LUNATIC I'VE MANAGED. WON'T BE THE LAST.
YOU NOTICE ANYTHING ELSE, TALK TO MAGNUM. I NEED TO TAKE A ROAD TRIP.

SHERIDEN, WYOMING.
GAS
CLICK

MR. PROSS? IT'S AGENT BREMBLE.
ONE WAY
HERE.
YOU CAME A LONG WAY FOR A CONVERSATION, AGENT BREMBLE.
EDEN IS A DIFFICULT CONVERSATION TO HAVE. WITH ANYONE. I DON'T MIND THE TRIP IF YOU'RE WILLING TO HAVE IT, MR. PROSS.
HAVE A SEAT, AGENT BREMBLE. LET'S TALK ABOUT PARADISE.

ISAAC SHIFFRON. YOU WANT ANSWERS ABOUT EDEN, YOU START WITH HIM. THEN YOU END WITH HIM.
Record
WHO IS HE?
HE'S THE WORST IN ALL OF US.
EDEN WAS HIS VISION. I WAS THERE WHEN IT STARTED. I BELIEVED IN HIM. IN WHAT HE SAW.
IN WHAT HE PROMISED TO MAKE ME.
MAKE YOU? MAKE YOU WHAT?
FREE. FROM ALL THE THINGS THAT HOLD US BACK.
BUT I BROKE HIS LAWS. I WAS BANISHED FROM EDEN. SO HE CUT OFF MY NOSE --
TO SPITE MY FACE.
YOU DIDN'T BLINK.
MAYBE THIS IS A STORY YOU CAN UNDERSTAND, AFTER ALL.

THIS IS IRREGULAR, US MEETING IN PERSON LIKE THIS.
WHO DID YOU SEND ME?
SHE KILLED THREE PEOPLE IN MY TOWN. WITH A FUCKING ROCKS GLASS.
SHE'S MY DAUGHTER.
YOUR WHAT?
DON'T YOU LOOK AT ME LIKE THAT.
YOU HAVE CHILDREN THAT COMPLICATE THINGS TOO.
HER MOTHER MEANT NOTHING BUT MOLLY HAPPENED. I NEVER TOOK HER IN BUT I KEPT CARE OF HER. FROM A DISTANCE.
AND SHE'S THE WORST THING I'VE EVER DONE TO THIS WORLD.

IF YOU WANT ME TO MAKE THIS GO AWAY --

NO, LAURA. I PUT HER THERE TO KEEP HER SAFE. IF YOU WANT EDEN PROTECTED THEN SHE STAYS SAFE.

I'VE GOT YOUR BLOOD MONEY, SCHULTZ. THAT'S MY INSURANCE --

FUCK THAT MONEY, SHE'S MY DAUGHTER. WHATEVER HAPPENS TO HER, HAPPENS TO EDEN.

AND YOU.

"JUST KEEP HER AWAY FROM WHAT YOU LOVE."
HEY THERE, DARLIN'.
MOLLY, IS IT? THAT SHORT FOR ANYTHING?
SHERIFF MAGNUM. I HEARD YOU'RE THE LAW IN TOWN.
AND I HEAR YOU HAD A LITTLE TROUBLE IN THE BAR LAST NIGHT.
GOTTA WATCH OUT FOR THAT TROUBLE. YOU PUT TOO MUCH OUT, AND IT'LL COME BACK TO YOU.
OH, DIDN'T MISS MAYOR TELL YOU THAT YOU CAN'T BOTHER ME?
I THINK THIS COUNTS AS BOTHERING.
JUST LETTING YOU KNOW THAT I'M WATCHING YOU. LIKE I WATCH EVERYTHING 'ROUND HERE.
WATCHING ME.
WELL, I HOPE I LOOK GOOD.

BLACK COFFEE, PLEASE.

I HEAR MARK LOVES YOUR COFFEE.

YOU HEARD FROM WHO?
PEEE-PLE. PEOPLE WHO SAY YOU SPEND A LOT OF TIME WITH HIM.
I THINK MARK'S INTERESTING.
OKAY, MOLLY --
I GET YOU. YOUR WHOLE "NICE AND CRAZY" THING. IT'S CUTE.

CUTE?
AS A BUTTON.
I KNOW WHAT YOU DID IN THAT BAR. THE MEN YOU KILLED? THEY HAD IT COMING BEFORE THEY GOT HERE. BUT BERTHA BEHIND THE BAR? BERTHA WAS A GOOD WOMAN.
I'M PRETTY SURE NO ONE IS GOOD HERE, MISS MAGGIE.
MARK IS GOOD. AND IF YOU COME NEAR HIM WITH WHATEVER CRAZY BULLSHIT YOU THINK YOU CAN GET AWAY WITH PULLING --
I'LL BREAK YOU, BITCH. RIGHT IN HALF.
AND I'LL STAND OVER YOUR BODY.

COFFEE'S ON ME.

BITTER.

MOTOR INN
VACANCY
Isaac wanted a place broken off from the weakness of government.
Of man's law.
We all believed in him. It felt like the dawn of a new world.
Play
We came into Eden on fire, brother. '69, '72, I dunno the year now.
ISAAC SHIFFRON
1969
Was before you could see the world on your goddamned phone.
Isaac cut that place off. Choked that town until it wasn't part of the world.
I hadn't seen anything like him since the war.
And that's how we took that town. Just like a dink village.

Everything you're seeing now. World tearing itself apart. Gods fightin' through children with bombs strapped on their chests.
Jesus, Allah, and the almighty dollar.
Isaac saw all of that comin'.
That's why he wanted to build a place where the weakness of the world couldn't touch us.
You don't know anything about that, do you Agent Bremble?
You're trying to take down a place you can't even understand.
What kin' of evil you seen, Agent Bremble?
Life ain't bit you.
How you gon' to break what Isaac built --
When you ain't got no scars?

HEY, MARK.
WHAT DID YOU TELL YOUR MOTHER ABOUT ME?
I TOLD HER YOU WERE A PREDATOR. A SHARK.
BECAUSE YOU ARE.
YOU'RE NOT AFRAID OF ME. MOST PEOPLE, WHEN THEY SEE ME--
REALLY SEE ME.
THEY'RE AFRAID OF ME.
IT'S BEEN A LONG TIME SINCE SOMEONE REALLY SAW ME, MARK. IT'S NICE.
I'M A PERSON COMPELLED TO BREAK THINGS WHEN I KNOW THEY'RE FRAGILE. YOU'RE NOT FRAGILE.
MY MOTHER WANTS TO KILL YOU.

A LOT OF PEOPLE WANT TO KILL ME. THAT'S WHY I'M HERE. WHAT DO YOU WANT TO DO?
WITH ME.
I WANT TO HAVE SEX WITH YOU.
BUT THAT'S ONLY BECAUSE YOU'RE BEAUTIFUL.
AND THAT ISN'T A GOOD ENOUGH REASON TO DO IT.
SO NOW I WANT YOU TO LEAVE.
ONLY PART OF YOU WANTS ME TO LEAVE. THE PART OF YOU THAT POURS COFFEE IN THAT DINER.

I'LL LISTEN TO THAT PART.
TONIGHT.
BUT I WON'T LISTEN FOREVER.
WHY IS THE SHARK FOLLOWING ME?
BECAUSE THERE'S BLOOD IN THE WATER.
AND I CAN'T RESIST THE SMELL.

WHERE'S MOLLY?
I TOLD HER SHE COULDN'T STAY IN OUR HOUSE. SHE'S TALENTED. SHE'LL FIND A BED.
WE NEED TO WATCH HER, LAURA.
WE NEED TO WATCH EVERYONE.
HOW DOES THIS END, MAG? HOW DO *WE* END?
I DON'T THINK 'BOUT ENDINGS, LAURA. I KEEP MY MIND ON RIGHT NOW AND THE FUTURE TAKES CARE OF ITSELF.
THIS PLACE WAS ISAAC'S DREAM. NOT OURS. AND WE'RE BURNING OUR SOULS TO KEEP IT.
WE CAN WALK AWAY, LAURA. PUT MARK IN THE CAR AND WE CAN JUST DRIVE. LET THESE ANIMALS SORT THEMSELVES OUT AND MAKE A NEW KING.
WE'VE NEVER BEEN GOOD AT RUNNING, MAG. WE'RE GOOD AT FIGHTING.
I JUST FORGOT WHAT WE'RE FIGHTING FOR. WHO WE'RE FIGHTING AGAINST.
AND HOW DO WE KNOW WHEN WE'VE WON?

BILL
"I LOOK AT MARK AND I SEE ISAAC IN HIS EYES.
"WATCHING ME.
BILL
"I SPEND MY TIME WAITING FOR MARK TO REALIZE WHAT HE IS.
"IT'S THE KIND OF THING THAT STALKS YOU, MAG.
"ALL THESE FUCKING THINGS CLOSING IN ON US. INSIDE EDEN. OUTSIDE OF IT.
"I JUST WANT TO STOP.
"AND TURN AROUND.
"AND TELL THEM ALL TO GO AHEAD AND FINISH IT."

YOU'RE FRAGILE, MISS MAGGIE.
AND NOW YOU KNOW IT.

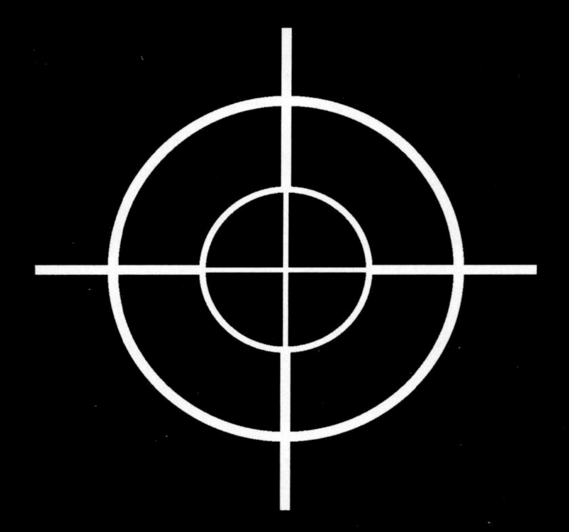

CHAPTER 11

HEY, DAD. YEAH, I'M FINE HERE. IT'S COLD AND QUIET.
REMEMBER BACK WHEN WE'D GO WALKING AND YOU'D WRAP YOUR JACKET AROUND ME? YEAH. COLD LIKE THAT.
FBI BRANCH HEADQUARTERS, WYOMING.
THEY'RE TREATING YOU OKAY? IF THERE'S ANY PROBLEM, YOU LET ME KNOW. I TOLD THEM THEY CAN'T EVEN LET DUST HIT YOUR SHOULDERS--
DAD, I'M FINE.
EVERYONE'S LOVELY. I EVEN GOT A LITTLE TRAILER UP ON A HILL. IT'S GOT THESE FAKE WOODEN WALLS. FUNNY FAKE WOODEN WALLS.
YOU GONNA COME SEE ME, DAD? I MISS YOU.
I'LL TRY, ANGEL, BUT I CAN'T MAKE A PROMISE RIGHT NOW. THE IMPORTANT THING IS YOU'RE SAFE.
YOU'RE SAFE THERE. YOU CALL ME EVERY WEEK, OKAY? EVERY WEEK. IF ANYTHING HAPPENS.
NOTHING'S GONNA HAPPEN, DAD. I'M DONE BEING LIKE I WAS BEFORE. I REALLY AM. I LIKE IT HERE.
EDEN IS A NICE PLACE. I'M MAKING FRIENDS. I CAN DO THAT, DAD.
I CAN MAKE FRIENDS.

"THE HEAD-SWELLING CAME DOWN. THAT'S A GOOD THING. WE DON'T HAVE THE RESOURCES TO DEAL WITH THAT HERE, LAURA."
"WILL SHE BE ALL RIGHT? MY SON WANTS TO KNOW IF SHE'S GOING TO BE ALL RIGHT."
"SHE MIGHT WAKE UP DIFFERENT. SHE MIGHT NOT WAKE UP AT ALL.
"TELL YOUR SON AS MUCH OF THAT AS YOU NEED TO."

YOU KNOW WHO DID THIS TO HER?
IF I DID, I WOULDN'T TALK TO YOU ABOUT IT.
THEY'RE BLUNT INJURIES. I'D SAY IT WAS A BASEBALL BAT. LOOKS LIKE A BASEBALL BAT--
YOU'RE NOT A DETECTIVE. YOU'RE A DOCTOR. STAY THAT WAY, TOLMACH.
IF SHE NEEDS SOMETHING FROM THE OUTSIDE WORLD, YOU JUST LET ME KNOW AND I'LL MAKE IT HAPPEN.
SHE NEEDS A SAFE PLACE TO LIVE, MAYOR. WE ALL DO.
THAT WAS THE PROMISE YOU MADE US.

I'VE READ THAT VOICES HELP. I'VE READ THAT THE MIND CAN HEAR VOICES EVEN WHEN PEOPLE ARE UNCONSCIOUS.
I WANT TO BELIEVE YOU CAN HEAR ME.
TO SAY THINGS IN MY HEAD BEFORE I SAY THEM OUT LOUD. EVERYTHING I'M SAYING TO YOU, KNOW I HAVE THOUGHT, MAGGIE.
I MADE MY MIND ALL WHITE AND DREW THE WORDS BEHIND MY EYES.
PEOPLE THINK THAT I DON'T FEEL THINGS BECAUSE I LOOK LIKE I DON'T FEEL THINGS.
I FEEL THINGS.
I HATE THIS TOWN, MAGGIE. I HATE IT BECAUSE IT HURT YOU.
I HATE MY MOTHER BECAUSE SHE LET IT HURT YOU.
YOU CAN'T TELL ME WHO DID THIS TO YOU. BUT THAT'S OKAY. SOMETHING IN EDEN WILL.
SOMETHING IN EDEN WILL.

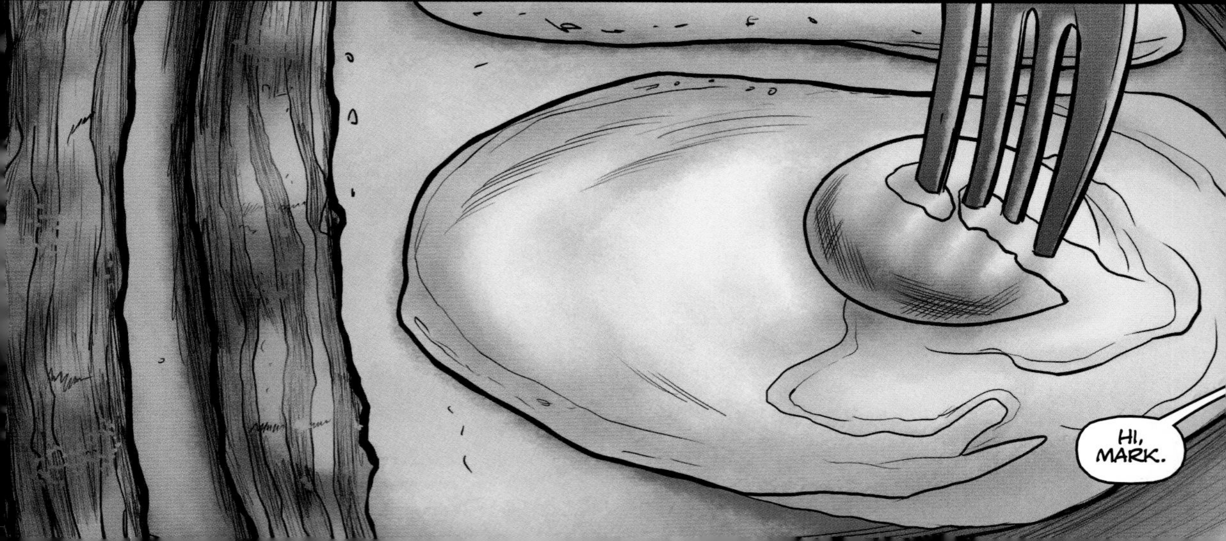
HI, MARK.

GOOD MORNING.
EVERYONE'S SO GLOOMY TODAY, BUT THE WEATHER'S GREAT. DON'T YOU THINK?
COULD YOU LEAVE ME ALONE, PLEASE?
WHAT'S WRONG?
SOMEONE ATTACKED MAGGIE LAST NIGHT. SHE WAS HURT VERY BADLY.
IS SHE DYING? SHE SHOULDN'T BE DYING. SHE SHOULD JUST BE HURT.
WHAT?

I DIDN'T WANT TO *KILL* HER. I'D HAVE *CUT* HER IF I WANTED TO KILL HER.

I JUST WANTED TO MAKE HER GO AWAY FOR A LITTLE WHILE.

WHY?

AH, I DUNNO. JUST HAD A FEELING SHE WAS GOING TO STOP US FROM GETTING TO KNOW EACH OTHER AND I'D LIKE TO GET TO KNOW YOU.
IS THAT HATE ON YOUR FACE? PEOPLE SAY YOU'RE A MANNEQUIN, THAT YOU NEVER SHOW EMOTION. THAT'S NOT TRUE.
I SEE PLENTY ON YOU.

THAT IS HATE ON MY FACE.
WELL, THAT BETTER *CHANGE.*

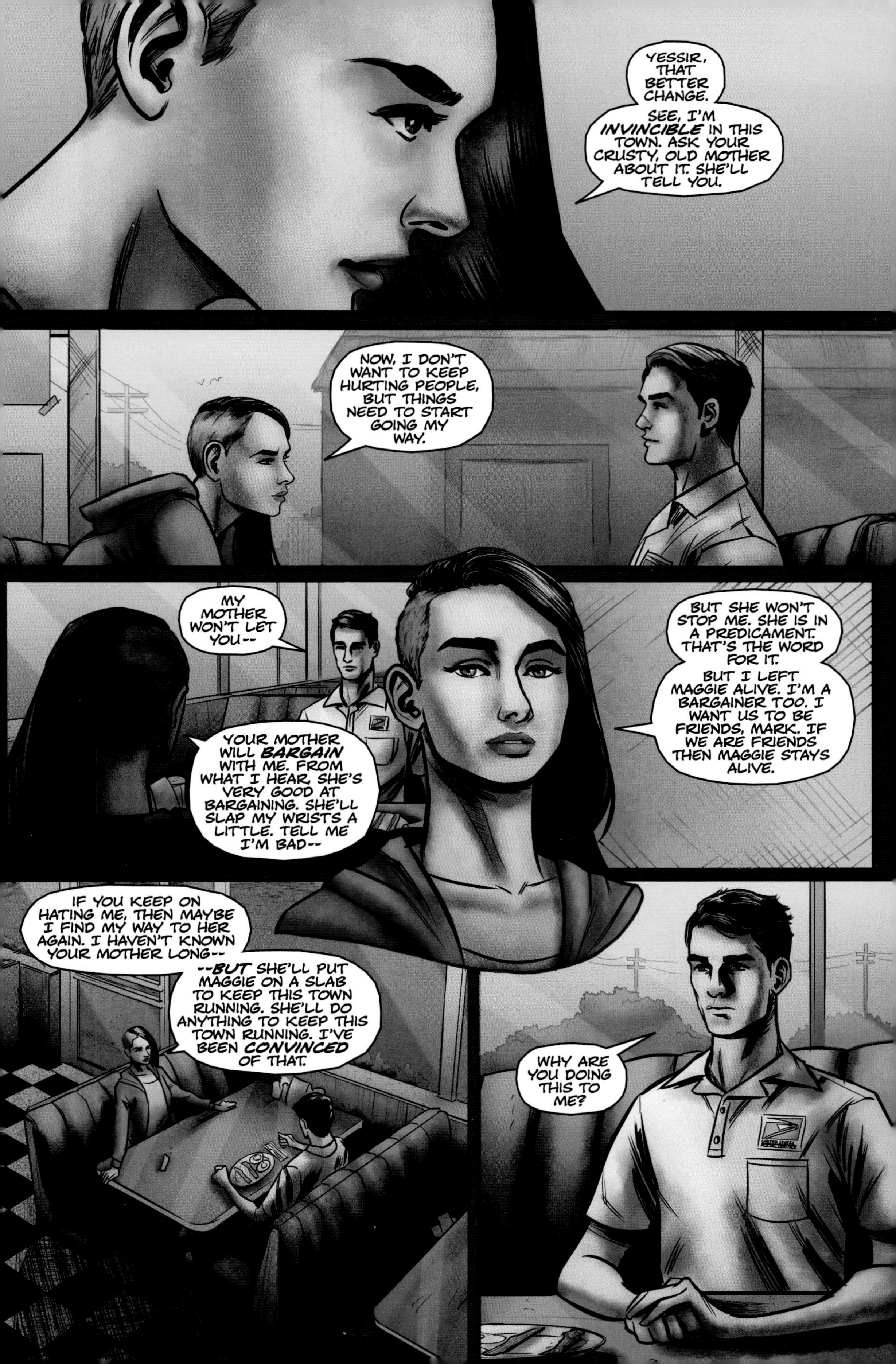
YESSIR, THAT BETTER CHANGE.
SEE, I'M INVINCIBLE IN THIS TOWN. ASK YOUR CRUSTY, OLD MOTHER ABOUT IT. SHE'LL TELL YOU.
NOW, I DON'T WANT TO KEEP HURTING PEOPLE, BUT THINGS NEED TO START GOING MY WAY.
MY MOTHER WON'T LET YOU--
YOUR MOTHER WILL BARGAIN WITH ME. FROM WHAT I HEAR, SHE'S VERY GOOD AT BARGAINING. SHE'LL SLAP MY WRISTS A LITTLE. TELL ME I'M BAD--
BUT SHE WON'T STOP ME. SHE IS IN A PREDICAMENT. THAT'S THE WORD FOR IT.
BUT I LEFT MAGGIE ALIVE. I'M A BARGAINER TOO. I WANT US TO BE FRIENDS, MARK. IF WE ARE FRIENDS THEN MAGGIE STAYS ALIVE.
IF YOU KEEP ON HATING ME, THEN MAYBE I FIND MY WAY TO HER AGAIN. I HAVEN'T KNOWN YOUR MOTHER LONG--
--BUT SHE'LL PUT MAGGIE ON A SLAB TO KEEP THIS TOWN RUNNING. SHE'LL DO ANYTHING TO KEEP THIS TOWN RUNNING. I'VE BEEN CONVINCED OF THAT.
WHY ARE YOU DOING THIS TO ME?

WELL, THAT'S THE QUESTION, ISN'T IT? WHY PEOPLE TAKE A SHINE TO ONE ANOTHER.
MAYBE IT'S THE WAY PEOPLE TALK ABOUT YOU. HOW MUCH THEY DON'T LIKE YOU. MAYBE I FEEL A KINSHIP TO THAT.
PEOPLE HAVE NEVER LIKED ME VERY MUCH.
LONELINESS IS A DAMN AWFUL THING. WORST THING IN THE WORLD.
BUT WE DON'T HAVE TO BE LONELY. NOT YOU AND ME.
YOU'RE INSANE.
PLEASE DON'T CALL ME THAT, MARK. PLEASE DON'T EVER SAY THAT.
YOU RISK MAGGIE'S LIFE WHEN YOU SAY THAT.

I'LL LET YOU FINISH YOUR BREAKFAST. YOU'RE NOT PLEASANT COMPANY.
BUT YOU'RE NOT FUCKING BETTER THAN ME. I CAN SEE IT PLAIN AS DAY.
YOU AND I ARE GOING TO BE FRIENDS.

MAZAR-E-SHARIF, AFGHANISTAN. FIVE YEARS AGO.
حضانة
I'M UP ON THE NURSERY NOW. NO SIGN OF MOVEMENT. GOING TO APPROACH.
OH, JESUS CHRIST... JESUS CHRIST.
I SEE THE BABIES... THEY CUT THE HEADS OFF THE BABIES.
FBI HEADQUARTERS, WYOMING. NOW.
THEY CUT THE HEADS OFF THE BABIES.
FBI
BANG

BLAM
BLAM
BLAM
"THAT'S RIGHT, AGENT BREMBLE. THE SENATOR HAS DECIDED EDEN ISN'T THE BEST USE OF YOUR TIME HERE.
"YOU'RE TO CEASE ALL INVESTIGATION INTO EDEN. IMMEDIATELY. THAT'S NOT ME TALKING, SON.
"THAT'S WASHINGTON."
YOU'RE PROTECTING EDEN. WHY?
EVERYTHING THAT PLACE TOUCHES WINDS UP BROKEN OR DEAD. THE RIGHT PEOPLE ARE AWARE OF IT AND WATCHING. YOU DON'T NEED TO STEP INTO THIS.
THE *RIGHT* PEOPLE.
LET'S MAKE SOMETHING CLEAR, AGENT BREMBLE. I'M NOT PROTECTING EDEN *FROM* YOU.
FBI
I'M PROTECTING *YOU.*
LET IT GO.
I HATE TO LET YOU DOWN, SIR--
--BUT I'M NOT WORTH PROTECTING.

NOT GOING TO DO ANYTHING TO HER?
I DIDN'T SAY WHAT I WAS, OR WASN'T GOING TO DO. I SAID I DON'T WANT YOU CONCERNED WITH THIS, MARK.
MARK, WE HAVE TO LOOK INTO ALL THIS. WE CAN'T JUST GO OFF WHAT SHE SAID TO YOU. PEOPLE SAY SHIT, SON--
I'M NOT YOUR SON.

OFTEN YOU HAVE ASKED ME TO TELL YOU IF PEOPLE ARE LYING. I HAVE TOLD YOU. YOU TRUSTED ME.
MOLLY *WAS NOT* LYING.

I WILL HANDLE THIS, MARK.

SHE WAS *RIGHT.*
YOU'RE *BARGAINING.*

WHAT? WHAT DID YOU SAY?
THERE IS A REASON YOU WON'T PUNISH HER. I WOULD LIKE TO KNOW WHAT THAT REASON IS.
I KNOW HOW YOU FEEL ABOUT MAGGIE. SHE DOESN'T NEED YOU IN HERE MAKING HELL FOR ME. SHE NEEDS YOU LOOKING IN ON HER.
SHE NEEDS HER BONES TO HEAL. SHE NEEDS HER BRAIN TO REGAIN NORMAL FUNCTIONS. SHE NEEDS ASSISTANCE TO HELP HER URINATE AND DEFECATE.
I NEED TO KNOW WHY YOU'RE PROTECTING MOLLY.
MARK--
YOU ARE NOT TO TALK TO MOLLY. WHEREVER SHE IS, YOU MAKE SURE YOU'RE SOMEPLACE DIFFERENT.
NOW GO HOME.
I HAVE ONE MORE QUESTION, MOM.
WHAT'S THE WORST THING MY FATHER EVER DID?

GODDAMNIT, GO HOME!
I UNDERSTAND HIM, LAURA. THIS AIN'T RIGHT.
MAGNUM, EITHER STAND WITH ME AND HELP ME--
OR LEAVE ME THE FUCK ALONE.

♬♬ INTO THE SEA OF WAKING DREAMS... I FOLLOW WITHOUT PRIDE...♬♬
♬♬ 'CAUSE NOTHING STANDS BETWEEN US HERE...THAT I WON'T BE DENIED...♬♬
HI, MARK.
WHY ARE YOU *INVINCIBLE?*

BECAUSE I CAN'T AFFORD TO BE INNOCENT.
THAT'S A JOKE. PAT BENATAR. DO YOU KNOW WHO SHE IS?
I HAVE TROUBLE UNDERSTANDING WHEN PEOPLE ARE MAKING JOKES.
I SEE.
MY FBI DADDY PROTECTS ME. HE'S SCARED OF ME, BUT HE LOVES ME MORE. HE PROTECTS ME. FROM WHAT I UNDERSTAND, HE PROTECTS THIS TOWN TOO.
AND THAT'S THE LAST I'LL SAY ABOUT IT, MARK.
I DON'T WANT YOU TO HURT MAGGIE, ANYMORE. I DON'T WANT YOU TO HURT ANYONE ELSE.
I'LL GIVE YOU WHATEVER YOU WANT.
WHATEVER IS A BIG, BIG WORD.

IT ONLY HAS THREE SYLLABLES.
HEE... HEE...
OH, WAIT. YOU WERE BEING LITERAL.
WHAT DO YOU WANT ME TO DO, MOLLY?

I WANT YOU TO STOP BARGAINING. YOU'RE NOT THESE PEOPLE HERE. I SAW THAT THE FIRST TIME I SAW YOU. YOU'RE BETTER THAN THEM.
FRIENDSHIPS DON'T START WITH BARGAINING. THEY START WITH TRUST.

YOU HATE ME BECAUSE I'M POWERFUL AND I TURNED THAT POWER ON SOMEONE YOU CARED ABOUT.
BUT WHAT IF I PUT THAT POWER BEHIND YOU, MARK? THINK ABOUT THAT. WITH ME YOU CAN BE FREE. FREE TO DO ANYTHING. SAY ANYTHING.
I WANT YOU TO TRUST ME. I WANT TO TRUST YOU.

AND THEN MAGGIE IS SAFE?

SHE'S SAFE UNTIL YOU DON'T CARE IF SHE IS. YOU HAVE MY WORD.
NOW PUSH ME. MAKE ME FEEL LIKE I'M FLYING.

MARK?

YOU ALL RIGHT?
THUMP

I'VE BEEN THINKING, SHERIFF MAGNUM.

WELL, YOU'RE ALWAYS THINKING, AREN'T YOU?

I KNOW WHY SHE'S INVINCIBLE. I KNOW HOW TO MAKE IT STOP.
BUT I NEED YOUR HELP, BECAUSE MOM WON'T HELP ME.

THE WORST THING YOUR FATHER EVER DID WAS MAKE YOUR MOTHER HATE HERSELF.
IF YOU DO SOMETHING TO MOLLY, YOU'RE CROSSING HER. YOU OPEN THAT DOOR AND IT STAYS OPEN.
YOUR MOTHER IS AFRAID OF PART OF YOU, MARK. I TELL HER SHE SHOULDN'T BE--
--BUT YOU TOUCH THAT GIRL AND SHE WON'T BELIEVE ME ANYMORE.
OKAY.
WILL YOU HELP ME?
GODDAMN RIGHT I WILL.

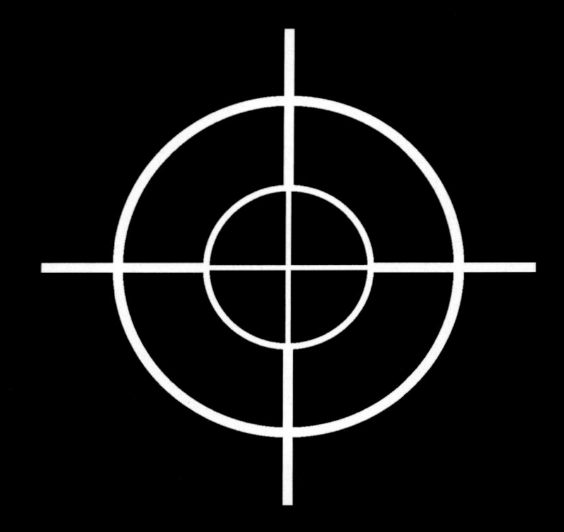

Chapter 12

WHAT DID IT FEEL LIKE WHEN YOU HURT MAGGIE?
DON'T WANNA TALK ABOUT THAT. THAT'S A SAD THING. I FEEL SAFE WITH YOU, MARK.
LET'S TALK ABOUT SOMETHING HAPPY.
DID YOU GROW UP HERE? LIKE, ONLY HERE? YOU'VE NEVER BEEN OUT OF EDEN, HAVE YOU?
IT WOULD MAKE ME HAPPY IF YOU HELD MY HAND.

TELL ME ABOUT YOUR FATHER, MARK.
I NEVER KNEW HIM. THEN HE KILLED MY SISTER. I NEVER KNEW HER EITHER.
THEN HE TORTURED ME AND HUNG ME FROM A TREE.
WHY?
HE SAID IT WOULD MAKE ME STRONG.
DID IT?
I DON'T FEEL STRONG.
MY FATHER HAS ALWAYS PROTECTED ME. EVEN WHEN I DO THINGS THAT UPSET HIM.
MAYBE YOUR FATHER WAS PROTECTING YOU TOO. HE TAUGHT YOU THAT YOU CAN SURVIVE. WHEN YOU LEARN THAT, NOTHING IN THE WORLD CAN STOP YOU.
YOU LOVE YOUR FATHER.
I TOUCH HER WRIST TO FEEL HER PULSE.
I WANT TO KNOW IF SHE'S LYING.
HE'S THE ONLY PERSON IN THE WORLD I'VE EVER LOVED. I WOULD DO ANYTHING FOR HIM.
THAT'S WHY I LET HIM KEEP ME HERE.
BUT I'M VERY GLAD I'VE MET YOU, MARK. I THINK WE CAN BE FRIENDS.
SHE'S NOT LYING.
AND NOW I KNOW WHAT TO DO.

IF YOU'RE GONNA JUDGE ME. SAY IT.
BUT MAKE DAMN SURE YOU HAVE A BETTER PLAN TO KEEP SCHULTZ WHERE WE NEED HIM TO BE.
I DON'T WANT TO FIGHT ABOUT IT, LAURA. I KNOW WHY IT AIN'T RIGHT. BUT IT AIN'T RIGHT.
SHE'S SPENDING A LOT OF TIME WITH MARK. WHAT IF SHE DOES SOMETHING TO HIM?
CHRIST, MAG. I DON'T KNOW. SCHULTZ IS PROTECTING HER BECAUSE SHE'S HIS FUCKED-UP KID.
AND I'M TRYING TO PROTECT MY OWN FUCKED-UP KID. I DON'T HAVE A PERFECT ANSWER TO THIS. NOT THIS TIME. YOU WANT TO COME UP WITH SOMETHING? FEEL FREE.
I NEED TO GO TO THE OFFICE AND EAT THE REST OF THIS GODDAMNED TOWN'S SINS.
AND THIS FELLA CONSIDERS THAT PERMISSION.

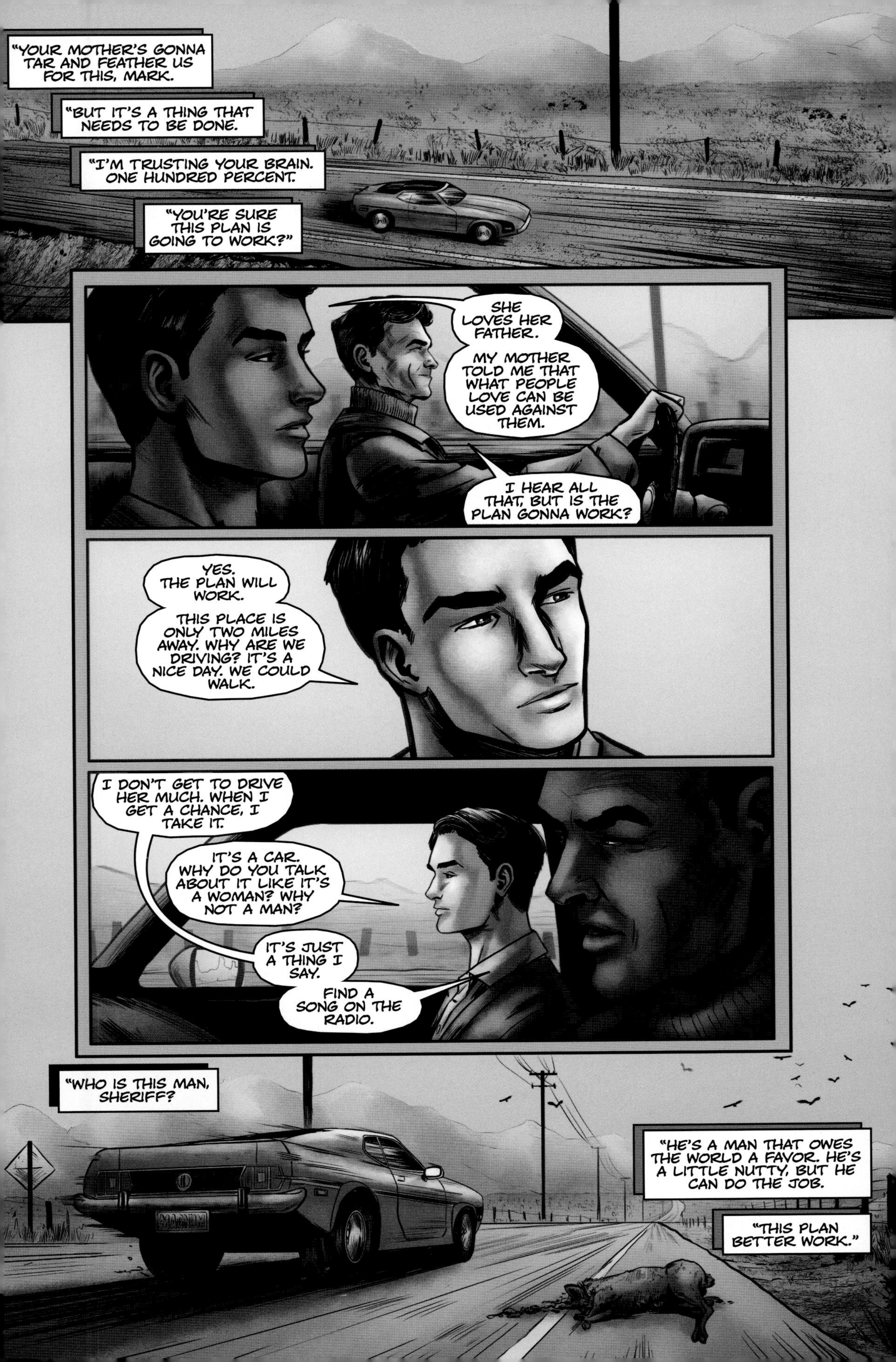
"YOUR MOTHER'S GONNA TAR AND FEATHER US FOR THIS, MARK.
"BUT IT'S A THING THAT NEEDS TO BE DONE.
"I'M TRUSTING YOUR BRAIN. ONE HUNDRED PERCENT.
"YOU'RE SURE THIS PLAN IS GOING TO WORK?"
SHE LOVES HER FATHER.
MY MOTHER TOLD ME THAT WHAT PEOPLE LOVE CAN BE USED AGAINST THEM.
I HEAR ALL THAT, BUT IS THE PLAN GONNA WORK?
YES. THE PLAN WILL WORK.
THIS PLACE IS ONLY TWO MILES AWAY. WHY ARE WE DRIVING? IT'S A NICE DAY. WE COULD WALK.
I DON'T GET TO DRIVE HER MUCH. WHEN I GET A CHANCE, I TAKE IT.
IT'S A CAR. WHY DO YOU TALK ABOUT IT LIKE IT'S A WOMAN? WHY NOT A MAN?
IT'S JUST A THING I SAY.
FIND A SONG ON THE RADIO.
"WHO IS THIS MAN, SHERIFF?
"HE'S A MAN THAT OWES THE WORLD A FAVOR. HE'S A LITTLE NUTTY, BUT HE CAN DO THE JOB.
"THIS PLAN BETTER WORK."

MASH.
PURGATORY IS MAKING YOUR MASH IN A DIRTY POT.
HELL IS WHEN THE 'SHINE TASTES OF METAL.
DALLAS.
WE NEED YOU FOR SOMETHING.
WOULDN'T BE HERE IF IT WASN'T IMPORTANT.
DONT TREAD ON ME

IF I'M TAKING OUT THE RIFLE FOR YOU, YOU'RE GOING TO OWE ME.
AND IF I USE IT, THEN YOU'RE REALLY GOING TO OWE ME, SHERIFF.
TAPES
I CAN DO WHAT YOU WANT. I'VE DONE WORSE.
AND I'LL KEEP IT ALL SECRET. I'VE DONE THAT TOO.
BUT I NEED A NEW POT FOR MY MASH. MOST EXPENSIVE POT I CAN FIND. NEW CORN. FRESH SUGAR AND STRAWBERRIES.
STRAWBERRIES ARE OUT OF SEASON, BUT YOU NEED TO MAKE THAT WORK.
HE SMELLS LIKE RUBBING ALCOHOL AND HIS HANDS ARE SHAKING. HE CAN'T DO THIS.
YOU THINK I'M NOT UP TO PAR, YOU LITTLE SHIT?

PICK SOMETHING YOU WANT ME TO SHOOT. DOESN'T MATTER WHAT IT IS. MAKE IT FAR.
THE BARN IRON OVER THERE, PLEASE.
THE BUNNY RABBIT?
THAT'S A ROOSTER.
IF YOU SAY SO, BOY.
CALL IT.
NOW.
BLAM
PING
I'LL SEND YOU INFORMATION ABOUT MY POT, SHERIFF.
AND FRESH STRAWBERRIES. FROZEN BERRIES ARE FOR SAVAGES.

"YOU WANTED TO KNOW THE WORST THING YOUR FATHER EVER DID. THIS MIGHT BE IT.
"THERE WAS A MINE BACK IN THE 1970S. WHEN ISAAC BROUGHT US ALL HERE.
"BEFORE YOU WERE BORN."
ISAAC KEPT IT RUNNING FOR A LITTLE WHILE. THEN HE DECIDED HE DIDN'T NEED IT.
SO HE LOCKED ALL THE MINERS IN HERE.
YOUR MOTHER AND I LET HIM DO IT. WE'RE STILL FORGIVING OURSELVES FOR THAT.
THIS WILL BE FINE.

FBI HEADQUARTERS, WYOMING.
"ARE THEY TREATING YOU WELL, MOLLY?"
I'M FINE, ANGEL. THINGS ARE QUIET.
Taking my stored leave
From: cbremble@fbi.gov
To: JSchultz@fbi.gov
This is a formality, but I've put in my request to take my stored up time. It's been approved, but I'm just letting you know.
Whatever you asked them to do to me, Schultz. They listened.
Bremble.
Special Agent Bremble
Federal Bureau of Investigation
Wyoming Office
Email cbremble@fbi.gov
I'LL TRY AND SEE YOU THIS SPRING, BUT I CAN'T PROMISE IT.
YOU'RE BEING GOOD DOWN THERE IN EDEN, RIGHT? IF THIS DOESN'T WORK OUT, I DON'T KNOW WHERE ELSE TO SEND YOU.
I LOVE YOU, DAD.
LOVE YOU TOO.
Are you sure you want to delete this message?
Yes
No
HE CAN'T PROTECT YOU FOREVER.
OH, MISS MAYOR.
WHO BELIEVES IN FOREVER?

FBI BRANCH HEADQUARTERS, WYOMING.
CHRIST!
CRACK

RIGHT TIRE.
PFFFT

PS-SST
YOU WANTED HIM SCARED? WELL, HE'S SCARED.
NOW GET OUT OF YOUR CAR AND SMILE.

SCARED THE FELLA. GOT THE PICTURES.
SIRENS ALREADY OUT. YOU'RE MOVING SLOW, DALLAS.
I'M EIGHTY YEARS OLD AND I CAME DOWN FROM A ROOF.
WE'RE FINE. WHEN BAD THINGS HAPPEN NOBODY LOOKS FOR AN OLD MAN.
YOU KNOW THE DEAL. YOU NEVER LEFT EDEN IF LAURA ASKS. YOU'RE THERE RIGHT NOW AND SO AM I.
NOW GET IN THE TRUNK, DALLAS.
DRIVE SLOW, YOU BASTARD.

I'M AFRAID, MAGGIE.

I CAN FEEL MY FATHER INSIDE ME. THE MORE I LEARN ABOUT WHAT HE IS--

THE MORE I UNDERSTAND HIM.

MARK?... HOW LONG HAVE YOU BEEN HERE?

YOU'RE PUTTING ALL OF EDEN AT RISK WITH THIS.
AND YOU LIED TO ME.
NO ONE LIED TO YOU, MOM. WE JUST DIDN'T TELL YOU WHAT WE WERE DOING.
YOU WOULD HAVE STOPPED US, AND MY PLAN WILL WORK.
IT DAMN WELL BETTER.
TAKE HER OUT.

"ARE YOU OKAY, DAD? YOUR VOICE SOUNDS STRANGE.
1

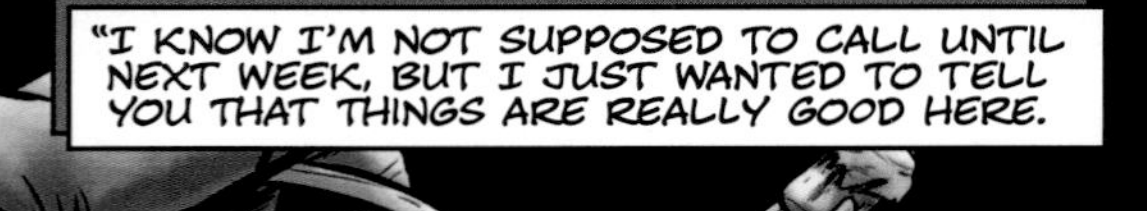
"I KNOW I'M NOT SUPPOSED TO CALL UNTIL NEXT WEEK, BUT I JUST WANTED TO TELL YOU THAT THINGS ARE REALLY GOOD HERE.

"I'M REALLY GOOD.

EVIDENCE
"YOU DON'T HAVE ANYTHING TO WORRY ABOUT. EDEN IS FINE."

OKAY, MOLLY. I'M REALLY BUSY TODAY. I HAVE TO GO.
LOVE YOU.
EVIDENCE
FBI

CLICK

MOVE ME TO THE OFFICE ON SEVEN.
THE ONE WITHOUT A WINDOW.

MADE THE CALL.
PLEASE DON'T HURT MY FATHER.
WE WON'T, BUT YOU HAVE TO KEEP MAKING THOSE CALLS. YOU HAVE TO KEEP TELLING HIM THAT YOU'RE HAPPY. THIS PHOTOGRAPH PROVES WE CAN GET TO HIM. I'LL LEAVE THIS HERE WITH YOU.
I WILL MAKE SURE YOU GET FOOD. AND CLEAN CLOTHES ONCE A WEEK.
I WILL MAKE SURE SOMEONE REMOVES YOUR WASTE FROM YOUR CAGE.
BUT THIS IS YOUR HOME NOW.
MARK, PLEASE DON'T LEAVE ME HERE.
PLEASE... I'LL BE GOOD. I PROMISE I'LL BE GOOD.
"MARK?
"I THOUGHT YOU WERE MY FRIEND."

YOUR MAGAZINE CAME. THE ONE WITH THE NAKED WOMEN IN IT.
JUST LEAVE IT THERE, MARK.
CLASSY BROADS

WE PUT THE WILL OF GOD ON THAT GIRL. NOW WE'RE KEEPING HER IN A DUNGEON.
YOU GOOD WITH THAT?

PEOPLE LOOK AT ME AND THEY THINK I CAN'T FEEL ANYTHING.
BUT I CAN FEEL THINGS. I CAN LOVE.
AND I CAN HATE TOO.

I'LL KEEP THAT IN MIND, SON.

SURE YOU GOT WHAT
YOU NEEDED.
DESERVED.
TELL HIM I GOT WHAT I DESERVED. THAT'S WHAT WE ALL GET, EVENTUALLY.
HE SAID YOU "OWED THE WORLD." I DON'T UNDERSTAND WHAT THAT MEANS, DALLAS.
DALLAS ISN'T MY NAME. IT'S WHAT I'VE DONE.
A LIFETIME AGO I MADE THE WHOLE WORLD CRY.

WITH THIS FINGER.

I STILL DON'T UNDERSTAND.
THAT'S BECAUSE YOU'RE YOUNG.
IF YOUR MOTHER LETS YOU DRINK, COME BACK NEXT WEEK.
I'LL HAVE SOMETHING SPECIAL FOR YOU.

MARK...
OH GOD.

TO BE CONTINUED...

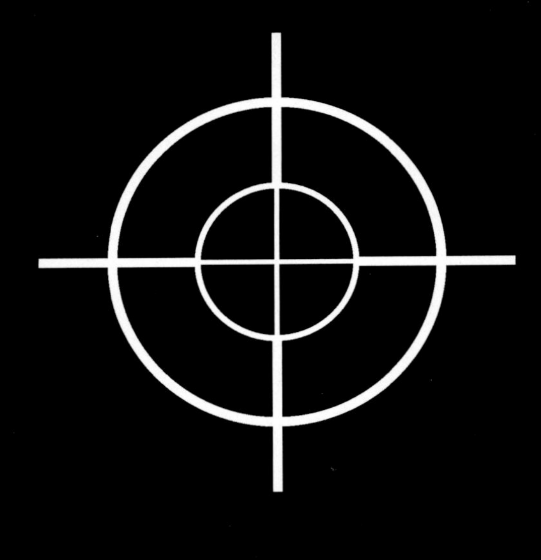

MAIL CALL

HEY THERE, POSTAL FANS!

Thanks so much for picking up this volume of *Postal*. It means so much to all of us here at Top Cow, and, as always, we ask that if you enjoyed this volume, please recommend it to your friends and put it on your pull list at your local comic shop! We love making this book, and we hope you love reading it, and we hope to keep putting it out for many, many issues to come!

You may have noticed a few changes to this volume, compared to *Postal vol. 1-2*.

Most prominently, **Bryan Hill** is now the sole writer of the series! While creator **Matt Hawkins** will still be maintaining creative input and assisting with the direction of the story, the reins have been passed. Don't worry — the mail will still come on time, and the residents of Eden will be as bizarre and dangerous as ever before. Granted, we've already seen some serious upsets in our favorite little Midwest town — and the violent Molly Schultz is only the first of them.

And speaking of violence — you may have noticed a bit more of it. Beginning with *Postal #10* (the second chapter in this volume), the series moved to a MATURE content rating. While this won't mean much in the way of drastic changes in terms of story or even the degree of graphic imagery shown, it does mean that the series will be reflecting the brutal direction that it's been headed down for a good long while. So if you thought this story arc was a little savage, you'd best buckle your seatbelt, 'cause you ain't seen nothing yet.

But we got plenty of fan mail and extras to get to before we can even think about *Postal vol. 4*. So let's get to it, but remember to bundle up, okay?

Wyoming is cold this time of year.

Happy reading,
Eden Postal Service
c/o Top Cow Productions

MAIL CALL

Our first message comes from Aaron who writes:

"Hey *Postal* gang,

Postal is one of the few series I look forward to every issue. I have thoroughly enjoyed your efforts to expand the characters growth in a multidirectional fashion. It's rare to find a story that is not constrained to the small world created by the artists. Life in reality pushes us in simultaneous progression. I love that the characters, especially Mark, reflect that same learning experience. Keep up the fantastic work."

Bryan says:
Aaron,

We always wanted Postal *to be a bit of a different beast. Change is constant and the things we endure alter us in ways we can rarely predict. As much as we can, we want the book to be about the evolution of these characters in ways that are organic to the story, not so much a pre-determined progression. I've thrown out whole scripts because what I intended just didn't make sense for what these characters have become and I let the characters guide me through the writing. Thanks for reading and thank you for writing. Cheers.*

Isaac says:
Thank you! I agree with your thoughts on the interesting character growth and I attribute all of that success to Matt and Bryan. Matt, firstly, created a group of really great characters. One of Bryan's biggest strengths is taking the characters' core concepts and figuring out what really makes them tick. That's what informs the story of Postal. *With this current arc, especially, I've been talking with Bryan a lot about the characters and where the story is going. Bryan is a VERY generous writer. He's even told me he's created characters for me that play to my strengths as an artist. If I have a setting in mind that I'd like to draw, Bryan works it in. And the GENIUS of it all is that his decisions that highlight my strengths are never at the detriment of the story he's telling. It still feels organic. And it is, because* Postal *is a true collaboration. As Bryan and I grow as storytellers and comic book makers, so do our skills — so does* Postal. *Thanks!*

Thanks for the kind words, Aaron!

MAIL CALL

Next up is one from Brandon C:

"By far one of the best comics I've ever read! The writing is genius and the art is captivating. Will we ever see a rebellion for the residents of Eden? Thank you for this story. I'm always wanting more!"

Bryan says:
Thanks for the kind words. I tend to think that the more you try and control a society, the more potential energy you build within it. When you base your power on fear and retribution, you're creating a system where power is the ultimate rule. The question is, how long will Mayor Shiffron be able to say the power rests with her? Stay with us and we'll explore that answer together.

Isaac says:
Hey Brandon! As a huge fan of the story, I definitely can't wait to find that out myself. I'm sure Bryan has something weird and twisted cookin' up and I can't wait to draw it...

Thank YOU, Brandon, for reading!

"Bryan and Matt,

Thank you for writing *Postal*.

Every now and then, a comic comes along that is so engrossing, so gripping, so excellently written, that you just can't wait of for every issue to arrive. For me, that is *Postal*. I adore Mark, I can relate to him in a way — he is an innocent soul, that while retaining his innocence, is very familiar with the darkness that is always very present in the world.

I feel like that sometimes, I've seen so much, experienced so much, yet I still fight to believe in the goodness of man. Having looked into quite a bit of humanity's darkness, I still seek to transmit what I believe in my deepest heart to my students: The world can suck IF WE LET IT. We CAN make it better.

Anyway, thanks again. I've told every friend I have about your book. I will continue to do so.

With Admiration,
David Wilkerson"

Thanks for letting us get to know you a little, David, and thanks for your kind words. In Eden, that kind of optimism is hard to come by — it's refreshing, to say the least. But let's see what Bryan and Isaac have to say...

MAIL CALL

Bryan says:

The world tests us all, and it tests those of us with empathy the most. I'm happy you relate to him. I do too. As we age, we trade our innocence for experience and hopefully we gain morality along the way. As Mark continues to look into the abyss of human experience, we try to constantly examine the effect of that on his character. I'm not sure if we are creatures of nurture or nature. I think the truth of the human spirit lies somewhere between the two. Ultimately, I do think we cannot control the evils of the world, but we can control our responses to it. Mark pushes himself to both understand the darkness, inside and out, while trying not to be tempted by it. We'll continue to address those issues in the story. Glad you're along for the ride.

Isaac says:

David, that's a fantastic and really insightful explanation of Mark, thank you. I think Mark is an outsider. He's stuck in Eden and he's really trying to make sense of the crazy world he's stuck in. Mark can be clear and articulate about what he wants at times, but almost every character with whom he interacts is trying to manipulate him for their own reasons. Mark is being pulled in many different directions at the moment and it's going to be interesting to see where he ends up.

Next comes this correspondence from Bruce:

"Wow!! I just stumbled upon this *Postal* series when I was browsing [through] a shop and picked up the first two issues cause I've heard some great things about it. Was a little hesitant at first but I flipped thru it and the art was amazing. So bought the two issues, got home.. read them.. and Holy F***!! It's sooooo gooood!! Called my shop to add the series in my pull immediately, and bought Issues1-7 First Prints on eBay right away. That's how good it was for me, the pacing of the series is really to my liking, it's really well done. Hope the series gain more publicity cause this is a great series, people just don't know about it. Hoping this series would be as big as Saga one day, in my opinion it's on par with Saga already, but yeah, Publicity. Hahaha! Keep up the good work guys!

from Alabama!"

Bryan says:

Bruce,

Saga *is brilliant so the comparison is very flattering. We've found that our readers have all come and stayed because they're invested into our narrative and that's the best any group of storytellers can hope for in the world of comics. Please keep reading. Tell your friends. Tell the internet and we promise to continue to do the best work we can with every issue.*

P.S. Yeah, Isaac is pretty amazing, but don't tell him I told you that.

MAIL CALL

Isaac says:

Thank you! I love the enthusiasm! And I'll tell ya, I just met Brian K. Vaughan at the last New York Comic Con recently and I gave him the first seven issues of Postal. *He was exceptionally cool about it and even seemed genuinely excited to read it! I wish you were there to tell him our book's as good as his, ha. I'm a huge fan of his (*Y the Last Man *is a masterpiece), so I really appreciate the exceptionally high praise! Thanks for the support! I plan on drawing* Postal *for as long as they let me.*

Easy on the praise, Bruce — these guys get to feeling too good about themselves, and the book might lose some of its edge...

MAIL CALL

BEHIND THE ART!

Let's take a look at how *Postal* comes to life by comparing Bryan's scripts with Isaac's layouts, to see whose vision is utterly destroyed first! Just kidding. But we thought you'd want to know.

For anyone who has ever wondered how a comic book comes together it is the culmination of several steps executed by various people over the span of several months. It all begins with the finalized script (which has undergone more than a couple revisions up to this point), that gets turned into layouts before the complicated process of final art gets underway.

Bryan and Isaac are prepared to peel back the layers of the onion and show you just how *Postal* is born... hold onto your butts!

PAGE FOUR

Panel One

On Agent Bremble's car driving a lonely stretch of Wyoming road. Near the highway. Not really rural as much as abandoned industrial.

Panel Two

On Bremble behind the wheel. Driving, looking serious.

Panel Three

Bremble pulls up to what looks like an abandoned gas station, one of those older ones and it has a workshop/garage built onto the side of it.

Panel Four

Bremble exits his car.

Panel Five

Bremble checks the load in his FBI issue 9mm pistol. (I think they have Glocks now. Not sure. I know it's a semi auto, but I'll confirm it for reference).

SFX: Click!

Panel Six

Bremble is slipping the pistol back into his holster (under his blazer) and walking towards the door of the gas station.

MAIL CALL

Notes from Isaac: One of the great things about working with Bryan is that he will often give me detailed descriptions of the backgrounds in the scripts. Bryan will sometimes talk about the mood and atmosphere in *Postal*, but sometimes I prefer to think of the backgrounds as other characters. Then I can think of the setting as being lonely (as Bryan states in his panel 1 description), dramatic, scary, safe, etc. Thinking this way helps me figure out what I'm trying to communicate.

Panel 1 - Because this industrial area is lonely, we wanted to show a lot of machinery to imply that it was once very busy on this stretch of road but has long since been abandoned. To emphasize Bremble's loneliness, I wanted to make his car very small.

Panel 3 - Sometimes I'll make a quick 3D model of a setting in a program called SketchUp. Using SketchUp is kind of like making cubes and shapes out of paper, but digitally. This program is especially helpful with realizing buildings at difficult angles or maintaining consistency with a background we see multiple times. It can definitely speed up the penciling process as long as I don't get stuck over-detailing the 3D model (which I have lost days doing!).

PAGE FIVE

Panel One

On Bremble entering the gas station. This is a visual reference to an old 1980's movie called THE HITCHER (which is brilliant by the way. C. Thomas Howell and Rutger Hauer). Bremble is sort of an antagonist, but I'm treating him like the hero of his own story. He's basically trying to investigate a criminal conspiracy so he's not a villain, he just wants to make life hard for Eden and shut it down.
Bremble's entering the gas station. It's dusty, maybe there's some venetian blinds and shafts of light. Ridley Scott shit, LOL. Bremble's entering cautiously, a little tight but he's not expecting danger.

BREMBLE: Mr. Pross? It's Agent Bremble.

Panel Two

Close on Bremble as he hears a voice from off panel.

PROSS(off panel): Here.

Panel Three

Bremble's POV. We see BECK PROSS(50's) standing at the dark end of the gas station. Old jeans and a thick sweater (it's always Fall for me in POSTAL, LOL) a sturdy man with a walking cane and a BLACK BANDANNA wrapped around his face. We can see his eyes. His balding, gray hair.

PROSS: You came a long way for a conversation, Agent Bremble.

Panel Four

Over Pross' shoulder. On Bremble.

BREMBLE: Eden is a difficult conversation to have. With anyone. I don't mind the trip if you're willing to have it, Mr. Pross.

Panel Five

Close on Pross.

PROSS: Have a seat, Agent Bremble. Let's talk about paradise.

MAIL CALL

Notes from Isaac: Since we won't spend too much time with this setting, I figured it was faster to draw these pages with perspective lines (those light green and pink lines). I'm DEFINITELY not as much of a movie guy as Bryan is and I have NEVER heard of *The Hitcher* and I don't know C. Thomas Howell or Rutger Hauer and sometimes I can get REALLY LOST when talking to Bryan! But! As per his request, I managed to find *The Hitcher* online and I'm glad I watched it! In panel 1, I tried to incorporate the type of lighting they had in that movie, and I'm very happy with how it came out. As an artist, it really helps to take your writer's suggestions and broaden your artistic vocabulary!

As for Beck Pross, I decided we should lose the glasses for the final inks. I was worried he might look a bit too similar to Director Schultz. I was a little sad about it since Pross here bears a striking resemblance to my dad, who also happens to be *Postal*'s #1 super fan.

MAIL CALL

PAGE SEVEN

Panel One

Establishing of an apartment building of a more metropolitan Wyoming. It's night. This is a safehouse. Not a a bad neighborhood but not one you would remember.

SCHULTZ(off panel): This is irregular, us meeting in person like this.

LAURA(off panel): Who did you send me?

Panel Two

On Laura and Schultz speaking in an unfurnished apartment. The safehouse where she can meet Schultz when she feels the need.

LAURA: She killed three people in my town. With a fucking rocks glass.

SCHULTZ: She's my daughter.

Panel Three

On Laura.

LAURA: Your what?

SCHULTZ(off panel): Don't you look at me like that.

Panel Four

On Schultz

SCHULTZ: You have children that complicate things too.
(linked)
SCHULTZ: Her mother meant nothing but Molly happened. I never took her in but I kept care of her. From a distance.
(linked)

SCHULTZ: And she's the worst thing I've ever done to this world

IL CALL

The script here mentions that this is an unfurnished safe house, sc
nd energy into figuring out the architecture and lighting of the se
apartment a loft with a sloping ceiling. I thought I'd get some mc
his way. I didn't want Laura and Schultz to just be talking in a hc

s two characters talking in an unfurnished room, I knew I could r
ge. So instead, I tried to make the conversation a little more inter
ers. Because Laura is being accusatory to Schultz, I wanted her t
he's closer to camera and in panel 3 she breaks the panel boarder
argument as she catches him in a lie, so I wanted her to feel large
e shadow.

MAIL CALL

SCRIPT TO ART FROM ISSUE #11

Here is a look at some of the process work from Bryan and Issac on *Postal* #11. Many of these panels have to do with Eden's newest resident — Molly — and how she is going to fit into the unique community *Postal* surrounds.

PAGE ONE

Panel One
Molly stands at a PAY PHONE at the edge of a town, main street. She's already in conversation.
MOLLY: Hey, dad. Yeah, I'm fine here. It's cold and quiet.
(beat)
MOLLY: Remember back when we'd go walking and you'd wrap your jacket around me? Yeah. Cold like that.

Panel Two
On Schultz, sitting at home, on the opposite end of the line.
SCHULTZ: They're treating you okay? If there's any problem, you let me know. I told them they can't even let dust hit your shoulders –
MOLLY (from phone): Dad, I'm fine.

Panel Three
On Molly.
MOLLY: Everyone's lovely. I even got a little trailer up on a hill. It's got these fake wooden walls. Funny fake wooden walls.
(linked)
MOLLY: You gonna come see me, Dad? I miss you.

Panel Four
On Schultz.
SCHULTZ: I'll try, angel, but I can't make a promise right now. The important thing is you're safe.
(linked)
SCHULTZ: You're safe there. You call me every week, okay? Every week. If anything happens.

Panel Five
On Molly.
MOLLY: Nothing's gonna happen, Dad. I'm done being like I was before. I really am. I like it here.
(linked)
MOLLY: Eden is a nice place. I'm making friends. I can do that, Dad.
(linked)
MOLLY: I can make friends.

IL CALL

This issue was a tricky one to draw because the entire issue is made
:ters. Dialogue can look very monotonous if the panels just show he
:s medium (which I love so very much) we don't have actors to deli
:mphasize emotion, so we have to compensate. With this page, as w
y with environment, composition, lighting, and fashion. All these "t
:an make a page look a bit more interesting and even introduce som
ater).

negative space and dismal lighting to highlight the lonely aspects o
is an outsider, and I wanted to show that in the first panel by drawin
It's dark out, but she doesn't mind. She's not scared of anything.

s will notice Molly's face in the last panel was redrawn before the p
rawing for me can be a real struggle — especially with close-ups. I
lined face before I eventually gave up and moved on to page 2. And
ometimes, however, the best thing to do is to get away from the dra
inks days later. Coming back to a drawing with a fresh pair of eyes

PAGE FOURTEEN

nnit, go home!

s up from the table.

of the kitchen.

agnum.

lerstand him, Laura. This ain't right.

m, either stand with me and help me —

e me the fuck alone.

IL CALL

:his page is pretty standard stuff, but I'm pretty proud of panel 3
into two halves: light and dark. Mark, in this panel, is literally tu
n has just rejected him and he is walking into the darkness. This
oned earlier. Bryan always writes amazing dialogue and I love i
v the feeling of the words. It's a wordless panel which I tried to
nto. Hopefully, this panel shows some foreshadowing of Mark's
ehind his mother's back.

PAGE FIFTEEN

trailer where Molly lives. There's a LARGE OAK TREE in front
ıd Molly sits on a swingset. This is a long shot. Picturesque. Mol-
are in silhouette against the bright sky.

; to herself.

e sea of waking dreams...I follow without pride...

on the swing. Still singing. She's not facing us.

ıothing stands between us here...that I won't be denied...

ing us.

·k.

ing in the grass, facing Molly.

· you invincible?

MAIL CALL

This page was fun because I got to design a weird background. The script had Molly on a swing and my idea was to have her over a cliff with a steep drop to jagged rocks. The cliff and rocks emphasize that both characters are one step away from becoming very dangerous. Molly flirts with that dangerous side of hers and swings back and forth. One moment she can be sweet and nice, and the next she is violent and ruthless. Mark is not swinging, but he too is very close to crossing the line into some scary territory.

Bryan and Matt and created these incredible, nuanced, fully realized characters. When the writing is this good, I have room to explore visual elements to highlight what I like about them.

MAIL CALL

Sheriff Magnum's Favorite Magazine —
He gets the issues a few months late, the poor guy.
Classy Broads. Vol. 3, Issue #17. 2016 November.

MAIL CALL

Anyway, back to the ACTUAL reader mail. This one comes from Del, who writes...

"I have to say this is an amazing comic. I've been meaning to write in for awhile now. We're so lucky that we live in a time were comics are beginning to be respected as a medium and seen as more than just super hero books for kids. Not that I have anything against those. I love comics in all forms. It's such a great method of storytelling and Postal is one of those books that really shows that. It's such an original story and the art is something else. I can almost see it happening. It sucks you in and makes you believe. The characters are real people with flaws, some way more than others. It makes you really care for the characters. I don't believe there's ever been a more unique character than Mark. The relationship between him and Maggie is done perfectly. And the suspense, let me tell you. I'm on the edge of my seat through the whole issue and then I'm left there waiting for the next issue. Also, I can't wait for the upcoming crossover with The Tithe. I have a feeling shit's about to get real. Hopefully, you can keep this book coming for a long time. Thank you."

Thank YOU, Del, for reading and writing!

Bryan says:
Hi Del. Indeed, the shit is about to get real. I love comics. It's my favorite storytelling medium and it's great that movies and television are bringing more people to the experience of reading them. I'm with you. We see all the characters in Eden as people, people with flaws and virtues and no one has to be perfect, or simply "good" or "bad" because no one in life is. I'm glad you like Mark so much. Mark needs friends. It gets lonely for him sometimes. The Eden's Fall *crossover is definitely something you're going to want to order from your local retailer. I can't wait to hear your thoughts about it.*

Isaac says:
Thanks for the kind words, Del! I'm so excited about the comics industry right now. There are so many new voices and types of stories being told and I'm really proud to be a part of it with Postal! The industry is more diverse and experimental than I can ever remember and more new, interesting voices are coming in every day. That means the market is welcoming to a book about a mailman, ha. Like you, I also really care about these characters. Bryan is great at a lot of things when it comes to writing and his ear for dialogue and characterization is unparalleled. Every day a new script comes in is a very good day!

MAIL CALL

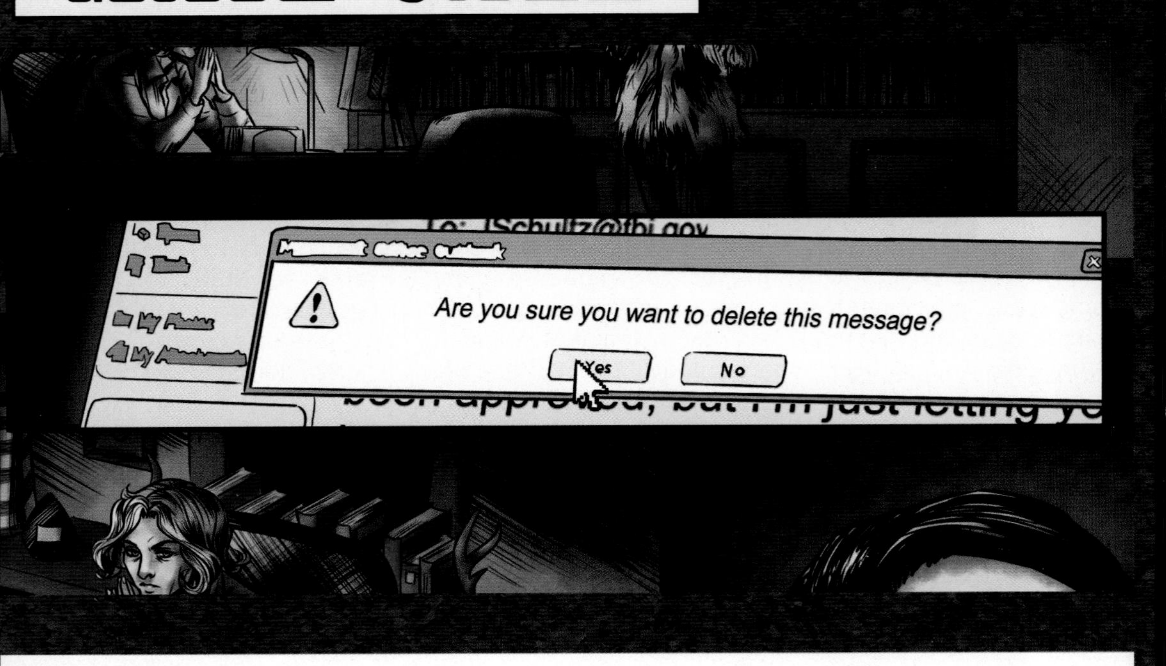

Next, from Gonzalo:

"First, all I can say is 'wow'...It has been years since a story has captured my attention the way Postal has and for that I say, AMAZING JOB!! This is a comic that immediately was added to my pull list and one that I itch for days before its release! My dream is to one day write a script of my own and stories like these really add gallons of gasoline to that fire. I'm currently packaging up issues 1-10 to send to my old shipmates overseas to spread the this story around the world. The most respect to everyone involved with making Postal a living, breathing thing. I am grateful for all of you!"

Bryan says:

Thanks, Gonzalo. One of the most awesome parts about writing is knowing that people all over the world are diving into the worlds you create. On this end, we're constantly talking about how to make the experience better and better for readers.

Your dream will come true the moment you start putting words on that blank page. Believe in it, keep fighting to get it in front of people and you'll get there. The only time anyone can fail is when they quit. You've got something to say, experiences to give people. I expect to write a letter to you about your book in the future.

Isaac says:

Thanks for mailing Postal, *Mark style! That. Is. Awesome.*

It means a lot that our work makes you want to write your own story. I know that feeling extremely well and that's why I'm here drawing Postal. *I was inspired by my favorite comics growing up and decided I needed to make it my career. It's truly an honor to me that* Postal *is that book for you. Best of luck with your own endeavors.*

MAIL CALL

Next, we hear from Alex:

"Hey there Postalites!

First time writer here! I just wanted to congratulate you on a great series. I especially like the covers and artwork. Whenever I find a new comic that I am not familiar with, like other fans I assume, I first go over the artwork to see if it's something that appeals to me. I really liked the cover for issue 8 and, after browsing through the pages (including the very last page with our introduction to Molly), I got hooked!

I guess my obvious question is where do you get your inspiration for the characters' back stories? Do you read a lot about real-life crimes for ideas?

Keep up the great work!"

Bryan says:

True crime stories are an interest of mine, mainly because I'm fascinated with the choices people make and how one choice can change the trajectory of an entire life. Postal *revolves around choices and consequences. I try not to think about crime as a concept, but as something that has a human cost on both the perpetrator and the victim.*

Isaac's art is what gets me excited too. Thanks for reading!

Isaac says:

Thanks for writing and getting hooked! I've always just assumed Bryan is a mad genius and in a previous life probably would have been a citizen of Eden.

And "Postalites" is my new favorite word, so we are going to just steal that from you. Thank you.

MAIL CALL

And Bruce writes:

"Wow... Postal's world is getting bigger and bigger... I really find the new character Molly to be quite interesting! I really do wish people would find Postal and Invincible stories on par with the big indie books out there... publicity is lacking a bit... Postal and Invincible are really underrated, but I really hope I can read this forever! :)
How about a guest cover artist variant... Fiona Staples perhaps? LMAO! Keep up the great work guys! Keep them great stories/art comin! Peace out! :)"

Bryan says:
Thanks, Bruce! There are so many good books out there asking for your money and time that it is easy for folks to miss stories and we're working more and more on making sure that people know about the book (and know how awesome our readers are!). If you like what we're doing, drop some Facebook posts and some Tweets. I've met tons of readers that found the book because a friend recommended it to them on social media. I love seeing every mention from people. All our readers matter to us. Man, I haven't been to Alabama in a while. I need to go back. Loved it there. Gorgeous, gorgeous place.

Now I have to call Fiona and ask her if she likes drawing crows. Wish me luck.

Isaac says:
Ah, thank you, Bruce! Definitely an honor to be compared to Invincible. I hope Postal ontinues forever as well. And actually, a guest artist on covers is really a fantastic idea. And of course, like the rest of the word, I'm a huge Fiona Staples fan. So, Fiona. If you are reading this, Bruce and I would like to formally invite you to draw a cover for Postal. Whaddaya say?! Bruce and I patiently await your response. Do you accept payment in the form of high fives?

MAIL CALL

And last, but not at all least, a letter from Patrick:

"Ok, (as common as it is becoming) this is the first time I am writing in to a letters page. I was a big comic fan when I was younger and got back into them again the last few years.

Postal is by far my favorite book right now. The writing is awesome. I love seeing the more mature themes, the characters who seem just a little off and discovering more in each new issue. It is something that regular superhero books can't give me. They literally have to tell the same story over and over. But with Postal anything goes, the story DOES move forward, there are repercussions.

And by far my favorite thing is the art. I can' really explain why, I enjoy the almost simplistic look, but the more attention you give a panel, the more detail you begin to notice. The heavy lines, the color, it is soooo good.

So ya, pat yourselves on the back. You convinced me to write in because you are honestly putting out a top quality book. Whenever I pick up my books and a new Postal issue is there, it's my first read.

Keep up the great work!"

Bryan says:

Hey Patrick. Isaac works incredibly hard to make every panel count. There's a real perspective in his artwork and a life that he breathes into all of the characters and the setting. The fun thing about creating Postal *is we're free to be more challenging, more extreme in our storytelling. I love superheroes and sometimes I think folks in Eden would be safer if they had one...but they don't so they'll just have to make due with me and Isaac, LOL. Thanks for writing!*

Isaac says:

Thanks a lot Patrick! I appreciate the kind words and I feel the same way about a lot of the current Image books. Image Comics, it seems, is taking a little bit more of the comics market share every year. That's fantastic news because it means the industry is growing and welcoming in new and different stories. We are transitioning into a more inclusive, exciting medium. I share your fandom and enthusiasm!

And thanks for saying the art is your favorite part. HA HA, take THAT, Bryan. I'M THE FAVORITE.

I do try to keep everything as visually interesting as possible and maybe even hint at a character's backstory with a clothing detail or an object in the background. So thank you for noticing! I really do appreciate that.

That's all for this volume — which means that's all for a couple months! But remember, Eden's not going anywhere — there are more stories to tell, and we promise there'll be violence, intrigue, and, of course, more mail.

Eden Postmaster
c/o Top Cow Productions, Inc.

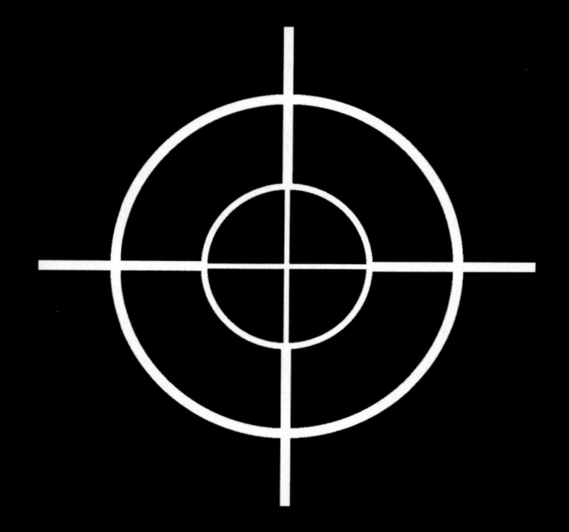

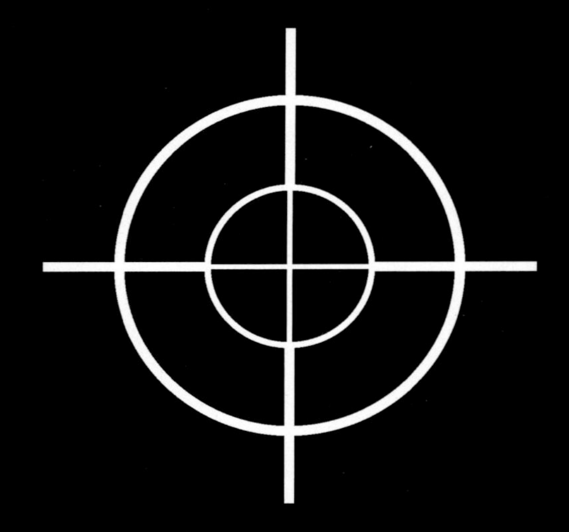

POSTAL #1
2ND PRINTING MEFCC COVER
ISAAC GOODHART & BETSY GONIA

POSTAL #9
COVER A
LINDA SEJIC

POSTAL #9
COVER B
ISAAC GOODHART & BETSY GONIA

Postal #10
Cover A
Linda Sejic

POSTAL #10
COVER B
ISAAC GOODHART & BETSY GONIA

Postal #11
Cover A
Linda Sejic

POSTAL #11
COVER B
ISAAC GOODHART & BETSY GONIA

Postal #12
Cover A
Linda Sejic

Postal #12
Cover B
Isaac Goodhart & Betsy Gonia

Meet the Creators

MATT HAWKINS

A veteran of the initial Image Comics launch, Matt started his career in comic book publishing in 1993 and has been working with Image as a creator, writer, and executive for over twenty years. President/ COO of Top Cow since 1998, Matt has created and written over thirty new franchises for Top Cow and Image including *Think Tank, Necromancer, VICE, Lady Pendragon,* and *Aphrodite IX* as well as handling the company's business affairs.

BRYAN HILL

Writes comics, writes movies, and makes films. He lives and works in Los Angeles. @bryanedwardhill | Instagram/bryanehill

ISAAC GOODHART

A life-long comics fan, Isaac graduated from the School of Visual Arts in New York in 2010. In 2014, he was one of the winners for Top Cow's annual talent hunt. He currently lives in Los Angeles where he storyboards and draws comics.

BETSY GOLDEN

After graduating from the Savannah College of Art & Design in 2012, Betsy began working at Top Cow Productions. Previously the Editor and Colorist for many of their titles, she now does freelance coloring work.

TROY PETERI

Starting his career at Comicraft, Troy Peteri lettered titles such as *Iron Man*, *Wolverine*, and *Amazing Spider-Man*, among many others. He's been lettering roughly 97% of all Top Cow titles since 2005. In addition to Top Cow, he currently letters comics from multiple publishers and websites, such as Image Comics, Dynamite, and Archaia. He (along with co-writer Tom Martin and artist Dave Lanphear) is currently writing (and lettering) *Tales of Equinox*, a webcomic of his own creation for www.Thrillbent.com. (Once again, www.Thrillbent.com.) He's still bitter about no longer lettering *The Darkness* and wants it back on stands immediately.